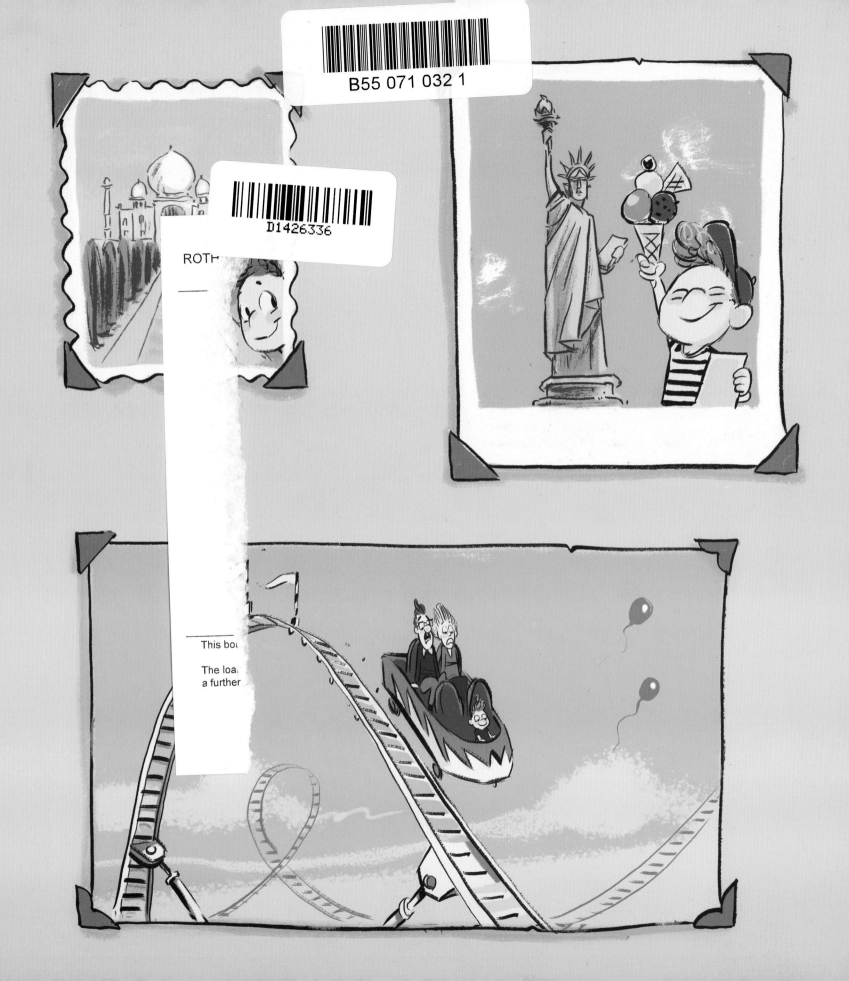

This bo

The loa
a further

For Adam, Sophie and Eva – with love.

First published in Great Britain in 2021 by Andersen Press Ltd., 20 Vauxhall Bridge Road, London SW1V 2SA.
Copyright © Adam Stower, 2021. The right of Adam Stower to be identified as the author and illustrator of this work has
been asserted by him in accordance with the Copyright, Designs and Patents Act, 1988. Printed and bound in China.
All rights reserved
1 3 5 7 9 10 8 6 4 2
British Library Cataloguing in Publication Data available.
ISBN 978 1 78344 654 4

The day FIN FLOODED the WORLD

Adam Stower

Andersen Press

In a house beside the sea lived a forgetful boy called Fin. Every morning he forgot to make his bed, brush his hair and switch off his lamp.

He always left for school without his **lunch box**...

And came home without his **trousers**.

Fin was a **VERY** forgetful boy.

But one night, Fin
REMEMBERED to
wash his face,

brush **ALL** his teeth

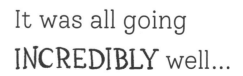

AND feed his goldfish, Jules.

It was all going
INCREDIBLY well...

...until he
forgot to
unplug the
basin
and turn off
the tap.

Oops!

While Fin slept,
The basin filled
with **water**.

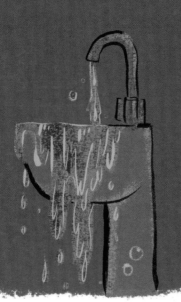

Then the bathroom
filled with **water**.

Then the bedroom filled with **water** too.

Then the house, the street and the village **ALL** filled with **water**.

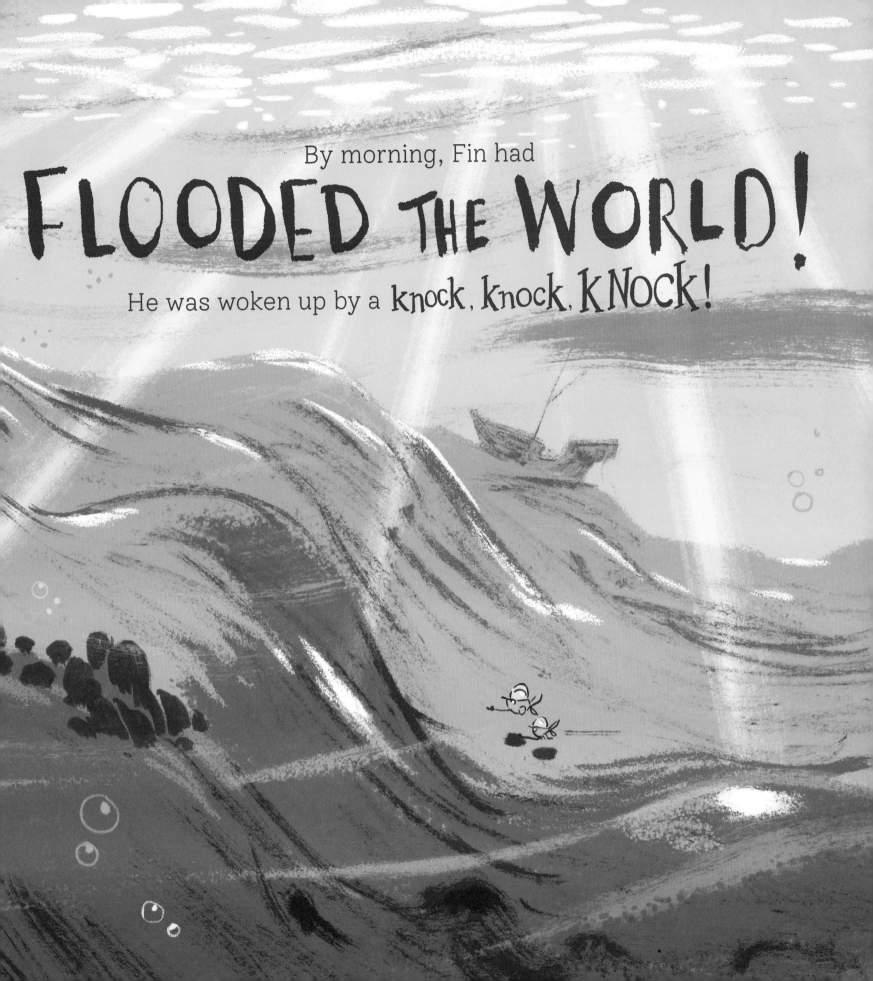

By morning, Fin had
FLOODED THE WORLD!
He was woken up by a **knock, knock, KNOCK!**

It wasn't the postman.

"Is your name Fin?" asked the big fish.

"Um… yes," said Fin.

"Did you flood the world?" asked the little fish.

"Er, perhaps," said Fin, looking around.

"**Come with us**," said the fish together.

Deep down at the bottom of the sea, Fin met a magnificent fish wearing a glittering crown.

"I AM THE FISH KING!" boomed the Fish King. "Is your name Fin?"

"Er, yes," said Fin. "Did you FLOOD THE WORLD?" asked the Fish King. "Um... maybe," gulped Fin.

HOORAY!

All the fish cheered, bobbing up and down and clapping their fins together.

"You're our **HERO!**" said the Fish King.

"Now we can go **EVERYWHERE!**

We can do **EVERYTHING!**"

And in a flash they swam up, up, up to the world above.

For the very first time, they had
lots and LOTS of un-fishy FUN!

And Fin, the forgetful boy who made it all possible, was rewarded handsomely.

He was given a seahorse to ride,

so much pirate treasure that his eyes bulged,

AND a whole **PALACE** to sleep in.

The next morning, Fin was woken up by another **knock, knock, KNOCK!**

It wasn't the milkman.

"Is your name Fin?" asked the big bird.
"Yes," said Fin.
"Did you flood the world?" asked the little bird.
"Yup, that was me," said Fin.
"**Come with us**," said the birds together.

Right up at the top of the ocean, Fin met a splendid bird wearing a glittering crown. "I AM THE BIRD QUEEN!" squawked the Bird Queen.

"So you are Fin, are you?"
"Yup!" said Fin, nodding.

"And you **FLOODED THE WORLD**, did you?" she said.
"That's right!" said Fin, beaming. "That was **ME**."
"Well," said the Bird Queen...

With the world full
of water, the sky was full
of **EVERYTHING ELSE!**
The birds had nowhere left
to fly. Fin felt **TERRIBLE**.
He took a deep breath...
and dived back into the water.

Fin knew he had to make things right

So he swam with all his might down into the dark blue sea and followed a tiny glowing light to find his village and his street and when he reached his little home he slipped in through the window…

...and pulled out the plug with a...

Pop!

With an enormous **whoosh,** **slurp** and **gurgle,**

the water swirled down the plughole as it all drained away.

Fin ran to the window.

The fish were back in the sea below and the birds flew high in the sky. It had worked! And everything else? Luckily for Fin, it all ended up **EXACTLY** where it had been before.